The Monster in the
Third Dresser Drawer

The Monster in the Third Dresser Drawer

and other stories about Adam Joshua

by Janice Lee Smith

drawings by Dick Gackenbach

HARPER & ROW, PUBLISHERS

Library of Congress Cataloging in Publication Data
Smith, Janice Lee, 1949–
The monster in the third dresser drawer and other
stories about Adam Joshua.
Summary: In a series of episodes, a young boy must
cope with a move to a new town, a new baby sister, a
new tooth, a baby-sitter, and his Great-Aunt Emily.
[1. Family life—Fiction] I. Gackenbach, Dick.
II. Title.
PZ7.S6499.Mo 1981   [E]   81–47109
ISBN 0–06–025734–2   AACR2
ISBN 0–06–025739–3 (lib. bdg.)

For Bryan,
who had worries and Jaymi.
For Jaymi,
who had fears and loose teeth.
For Jim,
who had all of us to cope with and did it so well.

TERRIBLE
BJECK

Contents

The Monster in the
Third Dresser Drawer

The Terrible Move

"I do not," said Adam Joshua, "want to move.

"It is not," said Adam Joshua, "my idea. And it is not a very good one."

"Nonetheless," said his mother, and she kept the move moving all around him.

She started the move in the attic. She took old clothes, and old books and a birdcage, and threw them down the stairs to where they landed in a heap at the bottom.

"Terrible," said Adam Joshua as a dusty army coat flew by.

"Terrible." He sneezed.

3

His mother kept the move going in the basement. She took old ball bats, and old golf clubs, and Adam Joshua's old baby things, and threw them up the stairs to where they landed in a pile at the top.

Adam Joshua ducked. A bear with one eye and one arm and no legs fell plop on the floor beside him. He tucked it under his sweat shirt.

His mother moved the move into his room. She took broken toys from his closet, and outgrown clothes from his drawers, and the collection of dried worms out from under his bed, and threw them with a crash into a throwaway pile in the hall.

Adam Joshua caught a truck with three wheels before it landed. He put it on the floor. Another wheel fell off.

"This still works fine!" he yelled. The bear fell out.

Adam Joshua started making piles of his own.

———

"I don't," said Adam Joshua, "like this at all. I don't understand why we have to move. And I don't think we have to really."

4

They were having strange things to eat. His mother called it cleaning-out-the-refrigerator. Adam Joshua called it something else.

He did not like cabbage.

He did not like beans.

And he was not partial to rhubarb.

But they were having them all the time, and every day, and sometimes all together.

Adam Joshua did not like his stomach confused.

"I, for one, am not going to move," he said each night as his mother tucked him in bed. She snapped out the light.

"I, for one, am definitely not going to," said Adam Joshua, all by himself in the dark.

———

Strangers came to look through his house. Strangers who might buy it.

"Keep your room neat," said Adam Joshua's mother.

"It's got bugs," said Adam Joshua to a girl who poked her head in.

He took all the things out of his closet and threw them on the floor.

He took all the things out of his drawers and threw them on the bed.

". . . and probably rats too," he said to the next girl.

———

"Good-bye," Adam Joshua's best friend, Peter, said.

"No," said Adam Joshua.

With Peter, Adam Joshua once collected ants from the backyard and put them in a shoe box to keep in the house.

With Peter, Adam Joshua once collected ants from the house, where they got loose, and carried them out to the backyard again.

With Peter, Adam Joshua was sometimes an astronaut, and sometimes a star commander, and sometimes Frankenstein, and once a germ.

With the move, Adam Joshua would never be those things with Peter again.

———

"Your new town," said Adam Joshua's mother, "is my old town. Where I grew up. I miss it."

"That's not fair," said Adam Joshua. "This is

8

my old town. I want to grow up here."

"Your new town," said his mother, "has your family. Your grandmother and your aunts."

"I don't want aunts," yelled Adam Joshua. "This town has Peter. This town has me!"

———

Adam Joshua stood on his toes and looked in the medicine cabinet. One time he drew a man with red teeth on the inside of the cabinet door. He used his mother's lipstick.

The man and the teeth and the lipstick were gone.

"It looks just like anybody's," said Adam Joshua.

The spot in the living room where he spilled milk and cleaned it with orange juice was gone. The kitchen drawer where he kept paints and a turtle was empty.

"Terrible," he said.

On the wall of his bedroom one time he drew around his foot with a pencil and made each toe into a face.

He wrote "**HEJP!**" inside the closet once when he was an outlaw and it was a jail.

He'd climbed a stack of chairs and drawn a tiny flag on the ceiling to show he'd been there.

Everything was gone.

Adam Joshua stood in the center and turned slowly around. It was nobody's. It was just a room again.

"This is a terrible thing!" he yelled. "And no one's doing anything about it!"

Adam Joshua found his father.

"I really hate this," he said.

"I know," said his father. "Moving is moving, and you can hate it, but that doesn't make it stop."

"I'm not moving anywhere," said Adam Joshua. "I'm stopping right now."

———

In the new town, Adam Joshua's grandmother and his aunts were waiting.

"Welcome," they said. "You're going to love it here."

"Bah!" said Adam Joshua.

In the new house, old friends and new neighbors and old family came to visit Adam Joshua's mother and father.

In the new house, Adam Joshua sat alone upstairs in a new room with boxes that weren't unpacked.

"Aren't those boxes unpacked?" an aunt said, sticking her head in the door.

"Never!" yelled Adam Joshua, slamming the door shut and pushing boxes in front of it.

He kicked his wall.

"Doesn't change a thing!" he said, rubbing his foot.

He put his hand on the wall and drew around his hand and drew a face on each finger. He drew two fingers crying and two fingers growling and the thumb shouting:

"KUNG FOOEY BJECK!" he wrote inside his new closet, on his new closet wall.

He looked at a map to figure out how to get home.

There were black lines that meant roads.

There were red lines that meant highways.

There were blue lines that meant rivers.

He closed the map and went outside.

Adam Joshua blew up a balloon and tied a knot in it.

"HEJP!" he wrote on the balloon. He

12

watched it when the wind came to carry it away. He watched it until the wind blew it far out of sight.

"HELP!" Adam Joshua yelled after it.

———

He lay in his backyard under a tree and cried. The tree dropped leaves on him.

"Enough," said Adam Joshua, and he got up and wiped his eyes, and then he climbed the tree.

In the tree it was dark and green. In the tree it was light and gold. Adam Joshua sat in the tree for a long time.

"Hello, tree," he said.

From one branch, he could see inside his bedroom window. Nobody was there. From another branch, he could see in somebody else's bedroom. There were Spiderman posters on the wall and Armand's Legion of Space Spies on the desk. Somebody sat on the bed, reading.

"Hello," yelled Adam Joshua. "I am Adam Joshua."

"Doesn't mean a thing," the boy shouted. He came to the window and slammed it down. He

raised it back up a crack.

"My name is Nelson," he yelled.

———

Inside Adam Joshua's room, on his desk, was a letter from Peter.

"I miss you," said the letter.

Adam Joshua took the one-eyed, one-armed, no-legged teddy bear from the box he'd packed and gave it a hug.

"I miss you, too, Peter." he said.

He looked at his hand on the wall.

"YEOW BJEH! (TERRIBJE)," he read.

"(MOVING IS MOVING)," he wrote beneath it,

"(AND THERE'S NOT MUCH YOU CAN DO ABOUT IT.)"

And then he sighed and put the bear on the bed, and began to take the two-wheeled truck and the other things out of the box and find a place for them in his room.

Amanda Jane Moves In

Adam Joshua had a new baby sister, but it wasn't his fault.

No one ever asked, "Adam Joshua, do you want a baby sister?"

They said, "Adam Joshua, a baby's coming! Isn't that nice!"

They said, "Adam Joshua, aren't you a lucky one!"

They said, "Adam Joshua, won't it be fun!"

No one ever stopped long enough to hear what Adam Joshua might say.

"Bluck!" Adam Joshua said at night into his pillow.

He knew all about babies. His best friend, Nelson, had one.

"Bluck!" said Nelson. "If they cry they get all the attention. If they smile they get all the attention. If they smell they get all the attention. You can't win, Adam Joshua."

Adam Joshua already knew that.

"It will just be for a little while," his mother said, moving his drawers, and shelves, and desk, and chair, and posters away from one side of the room and putting a baby bed and baby things there instead.

"Just until we get the baby's room finished," said Adam Joshua's mother.

Adam Joshua scrunched down smaller on his side of the room, between his bed and drawers and shelves and desk and chair, and glared.

His mother didn't notice.

"It may be a boy," his mother said, hanging a mobile with twirly things on it above the bed. "You'd like a baby brother.

"It may be a girl," his mother said, putting a

yellow stuffed duck up on the baby's dresser. "You'd like a baby sister."

Adam Joshua didn't think so.

"You're a big boy to share your room," his mother said, holding out her arms for a hug. Adam Joshua tried to hug her.

Where there used to be mother, now there was baby. Where Adam Joshua used to be able to get his arms around her, now he couldn't.

Adam Joshua put his arms halfway around his mother and put his head on her stomach. He could feel the baby moving around in there. It kicked him in the head.

"I think the baby likes you." His mother laughed, giving him a squeeze.

Adam Joshua rubbed his ear. He didn't think so at all.

———

Women came to give Adam Joshua's mother a baby shower.

"What a surprise!" said Adam Joshua's mother. She had made Adam Joshua help clean the house all day for it.

Adam Joshua poked around. There was a table

18

with a cake on it. On the cake were yellow frost-ing flowers and the word "Congratulations!" written in yellow squiggles. Adam Joshua took a taste of a squiggle.

"Adam Joshua, stop poking around," an aunt said from behind him.

There were presents wrapped in yellow and blue and pink and white. When his mother opened the presents there were sleepers for the baby, and sweaters for the baby, and booties for the baby, and baby toys.

Adam Joshua picked up a baby rattle and rat-tled it. He picked up a blue plastic cow and squeezed it. He picked up a small, cuddly, furry, warm, brown bear.

"Well, hi there!" he said to the bear. It was soft too, and smelled good. He gave it a hug.

"Adam Joshua, cut it out," said another aunt. "You're going to get it dirty."

———

"Any day now," Adam Joshua's mother and father said to one another.

"Any day now," they said to Adam Joshua.

———

"I thought you said day," he said when they
got him up at night, and took him in his pajamas
over to his grandmother's house. His father had
his coat on over his pajama top.

He had on one tennis shoe and one good
shoe.

"And your socks don't match either," Adam
Joshua told him.

Adam Joshua's mother waved good-bye from
the car.

"Don't get so excited that you can't sleep,"
she called.

"Don't worry," said Adam Joshua, going into his grandmother's house and curling up on the divan.

———

"It's a girl, Adam Joshua!" his grandmother said, giving him a shake and waking him up.

"Terrific," said Adam Joshua, rolling over and going back to sleep.

"Named Amanda Jane," his grandmother said, poking him.

Adam Joshua stayed with his grandmother for three days. For three days she told him things.

"You're going to have to be very quiet when you go home," his grandmother kept telling him.

". . . and very considerate," she kept adding.

". . . and act more grown up," she kept repeating.

When Adam Joshua got home there was a baby sleeping in his bedroom.

"Amanda Jane, meet your brother, Adam Joshua," his father said, holding the baby.

Adam Joshua touched her hand. It was warm and soft.

"Hi," he said.

The baby started crying, and then spit up, and then went back to sleep.

Aunts and neighbors and friends came all day. They brought more presents.

"OHHH!!" they said. "Look at those eyes!"

"AHHHH!!" they said. "Look at that hair!"

"Ahhhh," muttered Adam Joshua in the corner. "Ohhh," he growled.

"Finally, a girl," one neighbor said.

"Just what they always wanted," said another.

"OH, OH, OH. AH, AH, AH," sang Adam Joshua.

"Did you say something, Adam Joshua?" an aunt asked him as she went by. She looked at him suspiciously.

"Not a word," said Adam Joshua.

———

At night, Amanda Jane woke up three times. When Amanda Jane woke up, she woke up Adam Joshua's mother, and Adam Joshua's mother would come into the room and turn on the light and wake up Adam Joshua.

"Sorry to wake you up again, dear," his

mother said, yawning. "But this is what having a new baby is all about. We'll just have to get used to it."

Adam Joshua didn't get used to it. He didn't get used to Amanda Jane waking him up each night. He didn't get used to Amanda Jane crying. He didn't get used to Amanda Jane smelling.

He also didn't get used to always being told he was too loud.

And too babyish.

And too in the way.

"Adam Joshua," his grandmother said, "you're going to have to quiet down. The baby's sleeping."

"Adam Joshua," his mother said, "you're going to have to be patient."

"Adam Joshua," an aunt said, "we're falling all over you. Go outside and play."

"You can't win, Adam Joshua," said Nelson.

———

Adam Joshua got up one night and looked at Amanda Jane. She had on pink sleepers and she had her thumb in her mouth.

"Such a little princess," Amanda Jane's

mother said when they put Amanda Jane to bed. She gave her a big hug.

"The apple of her Daddy's eye," laughed Amanda Jane's father as he gave Amanda Jane a big kiss.

"Good night, Adam Joshua," they said, giving him a little hug and a little kiss.

Adam Joshua got out his red marker.

He crawled on his tummy on the floor under Amanda Jane's bed.

"**BJEH!**" he wrote on the wall under her bed.

"**AWFUJ!**" he wrote on the mattress he could see through the springs.

Adam Joshua looked at Amanda Jane. She was sleeping with her bottom stuck up in the air. She was wearing disposable diapers with plastic on the outside.

"**WIJJ BE JEAVING SOON!**" Adam Joshua wrote on the plastic across Amanda Jane's bottom.

Adam Joshua looked at Amanda Jane. He looked at the side of the room that used to be his, but now was full of baby bed, and baby toys, and baby presents, and baby. He looked at the soft,

cuddly, brown bear on the dressing table.

Adam Joshua took the bear and he took his scissors and he sat on his bed and started cutting.

The little bear was tough. On the body he had to saw the scissors a bit. The tail and ears came off with a snip.

Amanda Jane woke up and started crying. Adam Joshua kept cutting.

"Oh, Adam Joshua!" his mother said, standing in the doorway.

"Oh, Adam Joshua!" his father said, standing there too.

Adam Joshua looked down. He had pieces of brown fur all over himself, and all over the bed. Pieces of bear stuffing floated in the air.

"Baby's crying," he said, and he kept right on cutting.

———

Adam Joshua's mother and Adam Joshua's father held Adam Joshua and gave him big hugs and big kisses. They let Amanda Jane cry.

"We didn't know you felt that way," they said. "You should have told us. You didn't need to cut up the bear."

"Babies are a lot of trouble," said Adam Joshua's mother.

"Babies are a pain, sometimes," said his father.

"Babies are babies," said Adam Joshua, "but that doesn't mean you have to like them."

He looked at the bear pieces all over the floor and his bed and his feet.

"We'll glue it," he said.

While his mother fed Amanda Jane, his father gave him a hold and a hug and read him a book.

"Do you want to help me put Amanda Jane to bed?" his mother asked.

"Not tonight," said Adam Joshua. "Not yet."

After everyone had gone back to bed or been

29

put there, Adam Joshua got up.

He looked at Amanda Jane and pushed her bottom down so it wouldn't get cold, and covered it up with her blanket. He looked under his bed through bear stuffing until he found the bear ears and bear tail. He put them in the bed beside Amanda Jane so that if she woke up and got scared they would be there.

Adam Joshua went to bed and started to go to sleep.

"Good night, Amanda Jane," he said to his sister right before he did.

The Loose Tooth

"My tooth is loose!" yelled Adam Joshua. "And I don't know what to do about it."

"You don't do anything," said his mother.

"You wait," said his father.

"That's awful," said Adam Joshua.

Adam Joshua went into the bathroom and climbed up on the counter and sat with his feet in the sink to look at his tooth in the mirror.

He could push it forward with his tongue. He could push it backward with his finger.

He closed his mouth and pushed it both, back-

31

ward and forward, with his tongue. He could hear it in there in the dark.

Swish, swish, swish, swish.

He could feel it in there in the dark, too.

"Ouch!" yelled Adam Joshua when he wiggled it with his tongue.

"Ouch!" yelled Adam Joshua when he wiggled it with his finger.

———

"I don't want to wait," said Adam Joshua, finding his father.

His father was sitting in a chair holding Amanda Jane on one knee and trying to read a newspaper on the other. Adam Joshua tickled Amanda Jane and crawled up on the newspaper.

"I think it should come out now," he said.

"You think that," said his father. "But your body doesn't. You have to wait until it's ready."

"Waiting," said Adam Joshua, crawling back down and tickling Amanda Jane on his way, "is a terrible thing."

"String," said Adam Joshua's best friend, Nelson.

"We take a piece of string, and we tie one end to your tooth and one end to a doorknob and we slam the door hard and your tooth comes out fast."

"Sounds awful," said Adam Joshua.

"Nothing to it," said Nelson.

Adam Joshua found string while Nelson found a door.

Adam Joshua tied one end of the string to his tooth while Nelson tied the other end to the doorknob.

"The tooth will come right out and it won't hurt a bit," said Nelson, slamming the door hard.

"Yeow!" yelled Adam Joshua.

Adam Joshua went to supper, rubbing the sore loose tooth that was still in his mouth.

"Usually works fine!" Nelson yelled after him.

———

Adam Joshua looked at supper. It was what his mother called "combined casserole." That was not what Adam Joshua called it.

"I can't eat this," he said to his mother. "My tooth is loose. I can't eat."

"Too bad," said Adam Joshua's mother, taking his plate and putting it back in the kitchen. "Too bad your tooth won't let you eat chocolate cake."

Adam Joshua went to the kitchen and got his plate.

"I'll eat with my other teeth," he said.

Adam Joshua ate with his other teeth. Whenever "combined casserole" touched his tooth, it hurt. Whenever chocolate cake touched it, it didn't.

He brushed his teeth to get the chocolate cake off, even his loose tooth, even though there wasn't much chocolate on it.

"Getting looser," he said, wiggling it.

Adam Joshua started to go to bed, and got up, and went over to check on Amanda Jane.

Adam Joshua pushed Amanda Jane's bottom down and covered her with a blanket. He took her thumb out of her mouth and looked inside.

Inside Amanda Jane's mouth there were two new teeth, hardly used.

Adam Joshua put his thumb on the new teeth and wiggled.

Amanda Jane wrapped her tongue around his thumb and sucked it.

Adam Joshua went to his own bed and lay on his back. He started to go to sleep. He stopped going to sleep and sat up.

"What if I swallow you, tooth?" he said. Adam Joshua lay down and rolled over on his stomach and opened his mouth and put his face into the pillow so if his tooth fell out it would fall there. He couldn't breathe.

He lay on his stomach, and put the side of his

36

head on the pillow, and opened his mouth, and stuck his tongue out. That way, if his tooth fell out, it would have a ramp to roll down.

When he woke up the next morning, his tooth was still there. When he went to bed that night, and the next night, and the next, it was still there.

"What if it doesn't come out?" asked Adam Joshua.

"It will come out," said his father.

"What if it never does?" asked Adam Joshua.

"Trust me," said his father.

———

"Trust me," said Nelson. "Gum is sticky. If we chew enough, it will pull your tooth right out."

Nelson brought ten pieces of Bubble Bloobers and put four pieces in Adam Joshua's mouth and tried to put six in his own.

"Going to keep you company," said Nelson.

Adam Joshua and Nelson sat in the tree house in the tree between their windows, and chewed gum for half the afternoon.

"Watch this," said Nelson, blowing the world's biggest bubble.

"Me too," said Adam Joshua, blowing a bigger one.

Adam Joshua and Nelson sat in the tree house for the rest of the afternoon and pulled gum off their noses.

"Didn't do a thing for my tooth," said Adam Joshua.

"Terrible idea you had," said Nelson.

———

Adam Joshua stood on his head and kicked his legs while Nelson thumped him on the back.

"Didn't work," said Nelson, bending down to look in Adam Joshua's mouth and giving him a final thump.

"You can't win, Nelson," Adam Joshua said, falling over.

———

"Wait," said his father.

"Wait," said his grandmother.

"Wait," said one aunt.

"Wait," said another.

"A person," said Adam Joshua, "could get tired of waiting."

"Pliers," said Nelson.

"I'll wait," said Adam Joshua.

———

"Come out," said Adam Joshua to his tooth, wiggling it in the mirror.

"Right now!" he said, giving it a shove.

For breakfast, Adam Joshua had a bowl of Mate's Mighty Munchies.

"Munch, munch," went the cereal. *"Munch, munch, CRUNCH, munch."*

"Oh, no," said Adam Joshua.

———

"DEAR TOOTH FAIRY," he wrote, "DON'T BE MAD. I SWALLOWED MY TOOTH. IT WAS NOT MY FAULT. IT WAS THE MIGHTY MUNCHIES."

Adam Joshua slept with the note in his hand and his hand under the pillow. When he woke up there were forty-three cents there instead.

"I'm rich!" yelled Adam Joshua, waking up Amanda Jane.

"I'm rich!" Adam Joshua whispered to himself, feeling to see if he had any more loose teeth.

"It was the cereal," said Adam Joshua, showing Nelson the forty-three cents.

"It was just a matter of timing," said Nelson.

————

There was a hole in Adam Joshua's mouth, in between two teeth where his loose tooth used to be. Adam Joshua slipped his tongue in and out of the hole.

"Something should be happening," he told his father.

"Give it time," his father told him. "Something will happen. But give your body time. Wait."

"Wait," said Adam Joshua, going back to the mirror. "I can't believe it."

———

Adam Joshua waited. He waited a week, and then he waited more weeks.

And then, one day in one week, he climbed up on the counter and put his feet in the sink, and opened his mouth wide, and looked in the mirror.

Something was happening. Down at the bottom of the hole, where his old tooth used to be, was something little and shiny and pointy and white.

Adam Joshua very carefully put the tip of his tongue on it.

"Well, hi," he said, feeling the little, shiny, white point with his tongue.

"I've been waiting for you," said Adam Joshua, smiling at his new tooth.

The Monster in the Third Dresser Drawer

Adam Joshua had a baby-sitter.

Adam Joshua didn't want a baby-sitter.

Adam Joshua also had a monster in the third dresser drawer.

He didn't want that either.

"I think," said Adam Joshua to the baby-sitter, "that you are going to have to get rid of it."

"I think," said the baby-sitter to Adam Joshua, "that it is past time you were in bed."

43

"Monster," said Adam Joshua.

"Bed," said the sitter, and she turned off the light and walked out.

Adam Joshua lay in his bed, in the dark, and thought about monsters.

He didn't stay there.

He got up and turned on the light. He opened the third dresser drawer slowly and then jumped back quickly before something jumped out.

"Nothing jumped out," he said.

He went close to the drawer and looked in. He took his baseball bat.

In the drawer there were socks and shoe-strings and sweat shirts, but no monsters. There were T-shirts and undershirts and best shirts, but no monsters.

"Doesn't mean a thing," said Adam Joshua.

With one end of his baseball bat he lifted out all the sweatshirts, and T-shirts, and undershirts, and best shirts, and dumped them on the floor. He had to take socks and shoestrings out with his fingers, but he threw them down fast and hit them with his bat.

"I'll bet it's in the cracks," he said, taking the

empty drawer out and laying it on the floor, and getting ready to bash it.

"Hold it," said the baby-sitter.

She put the drawer back in the dresser and the clothes back in the drawer. She put Adam Joshua and his baseball bat back in bed.

The baby-sitter checked Amanda Jane, who was still sleeping, and glared at Adam Joshua, who was not.

"Now, good night!" she said, snapping the light off again.

Adam Joshua waited. Quietly, he wiggled out from under the covers and wiggled down to the foot of the bed. He wiggled along the wall with his toes for the light switch.

"Uh-oh," he said in the dark. "Too late."

The monster was out of the drawer and sitting on top of the dresser.

Adam Joshua could hear the TV. Down in the living room the baby-sitter was watching TV. In the bedroom a monster was watching Adam Joshua.

He wiggled his toes along the wall. He didn't take his eyes off the monster. It was a terrible, ghostly white, with terrible, awful ears.

"Hah!" yelled Adam Joshua, hitting the light switch with his big toe, and jumping back to the head of the bed, and throwing his bat, and pulling the covers up over his head.

He poked his head out.

"Oh, hi," he said to his stuffed white rabbit that was sitting on top of the dresser looking at him.

He got out of bed and put the stuffed rabbit, and the stuffed squirrel beside it, and the stuffed owl beside that, all into the closet. He slammed the door.

Amanda Jane woke up and started howling.

"You just come with me," the baby-sitter said to Amanda Jane, coming in and picking her up, and tickling her tummy and patting her back. "Just come with me, and I'll rock you awhile and sing you a song."

Adam Joshua started howling.

"You," the baby-sitter said to Adam Joshua, "get in that bed, and get quiet, and get to sleep."

"That's not fair," said Adam Joshua, crawling back into bed. When the baby-sitter turned out

the light, he closed his eyes. When she was gone
he opened them. The monster was in the corner
behind the rocking chair.

Adam Joshua wiggled out of the covers and
down to the foot of the bed. He wiggled his toes
along the wall for the light switch.

When the light was off the monster was there.

When the light was on the monster was gone.

Off—there.

On—gone.

Off, on, off, on, off, on.

He felt a hand on his foot. He felt hands on his whole body as he got lifted up and put back under the covers.

"And stay there," the baby-sitter growled, smacking off the light.

"You stay with that baby!" Adam Joshua yelled after her. "You shouldn't leave little kids alone!" he yelled, getting up and closing his door and turning his light on.

"**GO AWAY!**" he wrote on a white piece of paper with a red crayon. "**I DON'T JIKE YOU!**"

He took the note and scrunched it small and stuck it into the third dresser drawer fast. He slammed the drawer and jumped back in bed.

The door opened.

"This has got to stop," the baby-sitter said, turning the light off and going out.

Adam Joshua's foot started down toward the light switch.

"Now," the baby-sitter said, sticking her head back in.

Adam Joshua got under the covers.

"Stay there," the baby-sitter yelled from down the hall.

Adam Joshua stayed there.

The monster creaked open the third dresser drawer and crept out over the edge and crawled over to sit in the rocking chair.

"Couldn't read, huh?" said Adam Joshua.

Adam Joshua and the monster from the third dresser drawer sat in the dark and looked at each other.

The monster didn't say anything.

Adam Joshua didn't say anything.

The monster didn't move.

"Yeow!" yelled Adam Joshua anyway.

"What," said the baby-sitter, "am I going to do with you?"

"Nothing," said Adam Joshua. He looked at the rocking chair. It was empty. He looked at the third dresser drawer. It was closed.

"But why don't we leave the light on?" he said.

With the light on, Adam Joshua closed his eyes and tried to go to sleep. Every time he started to fall asleep, he heard the third drawer open and he woke up. Every time he woke up, he opened his eyes and sat up and looked at the dresser. Every time he looked, the drawer was closed.

He heard his mother and father come home. He waited while they paid the baby-sitter, and thanked the baby-sitter, and sent the baby-sitter out the door.

Adam Joshua waited until his mother walked into his room, carrying Amanda Jane, who was almost asleep.

"Help!" whispered Adam Joshua.

"There's a monster in the third dresser drawer," he said. "And it won't go away."

His mother put Amanda Jane in her crib, and covered her with a blanket, and patted her back.

She looked at the dresser.

She looked at him.

"I'll make it go," she said softly. "The third dresser drawer?"

"Yep," said Adam Joshua.

His mother opened the third dresser drawer and looked in. She nodded.

"Shoo! Scat! Skedaddle! Scram!" she yelled in a whisper. She wiggled the drawer and shook her fist and waved her hands.

"I think it's gone now," she said, looking in the drawer.

Adam Joshua got up and looked in.

"I think so, too," he said.

"I don't think it will be back."

"Nope," said Adam Joshua.

"Good night," his mother said softly, kissing him, and hugging him, and tucking him in, and turning out the light.

"Good night," said Adam Joshua.

"And about time, too," he whispered, turning over and going right to sleep.

Sunday Dinner
with Great-Aunt Emily

"Why," asked Adam Joshua, "does Great-Aunt Emily have to come for dinner all these Sundays?

"Why," asked Adam Joshua, "doesn't she just stay home?"

"Because," said his mother, checking the corned beef, "she's family, and she's lonely, and we like her, and she likes us.

"And why," asked Adam Joshua's mother, "aren't you dressed yet?"

"I don't like Great-Aunt Emily," Adam Joshua, getting dressed, said to his socks.

"She doesn't like me," he said to the knots in his tennis shoes.

Adam Joshua sat and pulled at the knots in his tennis shoes and thought about Great-Aunt Emily.

Great-Aunt Emily was old. So old that her bones cracked when she moved, and her voice whispered creaky when she talked. Old, old.

Adam Joshua didn't like old.

Great-Aunt Emily always wore black.

Adam Joshua always didn't like it.

She smelled like lavender perfume.

"Bleh," said Adam Joshua.

Great-Aunt Emily liked Amanda Jane.

She didn't like Adam Joshua.

"AND I DON'T JIKE HER EITHER," he wrote on the bottom of his tennis shoe before he put it on.

"Great-Aunt Emily's here," his mother called up the stairs.

"Great-Aunt Emily's here," Adam Joshua muttered to himself, going down them.

———

Great-Aunt Emily stood by the front door smiling. She had false teeth because her own wore out, and a hearing aid because she couldn't hear well, and a cane because she couldn't walk well, and glasses because she couldn't see.

"You'd better watch her," Adam Joshua's best friend, Nelson, always said. "She's falling to pieces.

"My Great-Aunt Jess," Nelson always said right after, "is all put together with her own things and everything works fine.

"My Great-Aunt Jess," Nelson always said, "smells like horses because she rides them, and dogs because she raises them, and tacos because that's what she cooks."

Great-Aunt Emily leaned down for a kiss. Adam Joshua clenched his teeth. When she hugged him, something poked him in the back.

"It's a gift, Adam Joshua," she whispered, holding up a package. "For you, for later."

When Great-Aunt Emily wasn't looking, Adam

Joshua picked up the package. He pinched it and poked it. It was wrapped in old brown paper and crackling yellow tape.

Nelson's Great-Aunt Jess gave him posters of spaceships, and brought him fossils, and one time caught him a rabbit.

Adam Joshua's Great-Aunt Emily had never given him anything before, and now that she had, it was something old.

"And nothing good," said Adam Joshua as he put it down again.

———

At dinner, Amanda Jane threw her vegetables on the floor.

"Such a sweet baby." Great-Aunt Emily smiled.

At dinner, Adam Joshua dropped his spoon, and dropped his fork, and fell off his chair.

"Boys are noisy," Great-Aunt Emily whispered to his mother, not smiling.

At dinner, Adam Joshua watched Great-Aunt Emily to see if her teeth stayed in.

After dinner, Adam Joshua and his mother did the dishes.

"She hates me," said Adam Joshua, handing his mother the leftover cabbage to throw away.

His mother put it in the refrigerator instead.

"Sometimes," his mother said, "old people don't understand young people. Sometimes," she said, "young people don't understand old. Sometimes," his mother said, giving him a hug, "everybody needs to try harder."

After dinner, Adam Joshua helped his father wash dinner off Amanda Jane and change her diapers.

"She loves Amanda Jane," said Adam Joshua. "But she hates me."

"Babies are easy to love," said his father. "Because they let you know how they feel. If they're mad at you, they cry. If you've made them happy, they smile and laugh. A baby will love you no matter what you look like or act like as long as you show it you love it."

"Babies don't know much," said Adam Joshua, tickling Amanda Jane's stomach.

"More than most of us," said his father, tickling Adam Joshua.

Adam Joshua's mother put on Great-Aunt Emily's favorite music. It was too slow and too loud.

"My Great-Aunt Jess," Nelson always said, "discos."

"Lovely," said Great-Aunt Emily, rocking Amanda Jane slow, to the music.

Great-Aunt Emily played checkers with Adam Joshua's father. His father let her win.

"That's terrible," Adam Joshua said, listening, from up in his room.

Up in his room, Adam Joshua killed off his Armand's Legion of Space Spies.

"Bam, bleep, zam, zip!" he yelled.

"Come play!" someone yelled from outside.

Nelson was in the tree house in the tree between their windows.

"I can't," said Adam Joshua. "My aunt."

"Aunts are aunts," sang Nelson. "And some are better than others."

"And there's not much you can do-o-o about it," Adam Joshua sang back.

"Come downstairs," called Adam Joshua's mother.

"You can't win, Adam Joshua," Nelson yelled after him.

———

"Adam Joshua," said Great-Aunt Emily, "bring me the package now."

"Bam, bleep, zam, zip," thought Adam Joshua, but he didn't say a word out loud.

"This is something," said Great-Aunt Emily, "that's been in our family for a long time." She took off the brown paper.

"This is something," she said, holding up an old picture of people, "that I'd like you to have now, because you're growing up."

Adam Joshua looked at the people. They were outside working, and they were wearing old, funny clothes. There were dogs and horses and chickens and children. There was a strange house in the middle that looked like it was made out of dirt.

"It *is* dirt," said his aunt. "In Kansas, it was called a sod house and it was made out of dirt

63

because people needed houses and it wasn't easy to get wood there.

"That's my mother," she said, pointing to a mother. "That's your grandfather," she said, pointing to a boy who looked like Adam Joshua, with two missing front teeth and a stocking cap pulled down over one eye. "And that's me," said Great-Aunt Emily.

Adam Joshua looked at the girl who was Great-Aunt Emily.

"Are those your real teeth?" he asked.

Adam Joshua sat on the chair beside Great-Aunt Emily and she told him about Kansas and sod houses. She told him about his grandfather as a boy, and about herself as a girl.

"My real teeth," she said.

She told him about the last of the Indians and the last of the cowboys and about going buffalo hunting alone and getting lost so that everyone else had to go Emily hunting.

"As a little girl"—she laughed—"I was an exasperation."

"I know exactly what you mean." Adam Joshua laughed with her.

"Would you like to see the ring my father made for me out of buffalo bone?" asked Great-Aunt Emily.

"Would you like to see my Armand's Legion of Space Spies?" asked Adam Joshua.

The more Great-Aunt Emily talked, the more Adam Joshua got to know his family in the picture. The more Great-Aunt Emily talked, the more Adam Joshua got to know Great-Aunt Emily, and the more she got to know Adam Joshua.

Amanda Jane tried to crawl up to get the picture.

"Put that baby to bed," said Adam Joshua. "She's too little to understand."

———

"Don't go," said Adam Joshua.

"I'll be back," said Great-Aunt Emily.

"You know things," he said, giving her a hug, "that I need to know."

"Yes," said Great-Aunt Emily, hugging him too.

———

In his room, Adam Joshua took the Space Spies off his desk and put the picture there instead.

"Later," he yelled out the window to Nelson. "I have something to do first. Sometimes you *can* win, Nelson," Adam Joshua shouted.

Adam Joshua got out paper to make a sign for the picture.

"FAMILY IS FAMILY," he wrote on the paper. "FROM MY GREAT-AUNT EMILY."

"And friends are friends," he said, going out to meet Nelson.

"And everybody needs everybody," he said, stopping to give Amanda Jane a kiss on his way by.

Amanda Jane
Moves Out

"It's her or me," said Adam Joshua. "You're going to have to choose.

"She's all over my room and into my things," he said. "She's going to have to go."

"Hold on," said his father. "You don't get rid of babies. She's here to stay. But her room's almost finished and we'll move her into it soon."

"We've been working on it hard," said his mother.

"Work harder," said Adam Joshua.

Adam Joshua's mother and father worked harder. They started early in the mornings and they worked late at night.

"But you're going to have to watch Amanda Jane for us," said his mother, washing out a paintbrush. "She gets into too many things that are dangerous, and slows us down. If you want us to hurry you'll have to help."

"I can't believe it," said Adam Joshua, catching Amanda Jane, and putting her in her stroller, and taking her outside.

Outside, Adam Joshua pushed Amanda Jane up one side of the street and down the other and started all over again.

Amanda Jane cried.

Adam Joshua sang her a song.

"Oh, some days you can win and some days you can't." Adam Joshua sang loud so she could hear him.

Amanda Jane kept crying.

"What's all that racket?" called Nelson.

"Come out," Adam Joshua called back.

"I can't," said Nelson. "My baby brother."

"I know exactly what you mean," said Adam Joshua.

Adam Joshua took Amanda Jane out of her stroller and carried her into the backyard.

"Look," he said, putting her down. "Flowers. Those are flowers.

"That was a petunia," said Adam Joshua, taking it out of Amanda Jane's mouth.

"Sometimes," Adam Joshua said, lying on his back and looking at the clouds and letting Amanda Jane crawl over him, "you're more trouble than you're worth."

That night Amanda Jane woke up crying and woke up Adam Joshua.

"It's either a nightmare . . ." said his mother.

". . . or something she ate," said his father.

"She ate two daisies and a petunia," said Adam Joshua, pulling the pillow over his head.

After his mother left and his father left, Amanda Jane kept sniffling.

Adam Joshua ignored her.

Amanda Jane started to whimper.

Adam Joshua ignored her.

Amanda Jane started to cry all over again.

"Oh, Amanda Jane," sighed Adam Joshua, getting out of bed. He got out his red marker, and drew a picture of himself on the wall above Amanda Jane's bed.

"Now you don't have to be afraid," he said, patting Amanda Jane on the back until she went to sleep again.

"Now everything's OK," said Adam Joshua, going back to sleep himself.

———

In the morning, Adam Joshua looked in Amanda Jane's room. There were buckets of paint, and packages of wallpaper paste, and snips of curtains, and swatches of carpet. There were Adam Joshua's parents sitting in the middle of it all drinking coffee.

"Break time," said his father, pouring more coffee.

"Work time," said Adam Joshua.

Adam Joshua used his own paintbrush and wrote "**AMANDA JANE**" across the wall in yellow paint.

"Looks fine," said his mother. "But that wall is going to be papered."

"Doesn't matter," said Adam Joshua. "Underneath it all she'll know it's hers."

Amanda Jane crawled into the room and into the paint.

"Adam Joshua," said his mother, washing paint off Amanda Jane.

"I know. I know," said Adam Joshua, carrying her back outside.

"Baby sisters," said Adam Joshua, "are a pain and a bother.

"My baby sister," said Adam Joshua, "is a pill and a pest."

"You said it, Adam Joshua," said Nelson, "and my baby brother is exactly the same way."

Adam Joshua told Amanda Jane not to eat sand, and not to eat flowers, and not to eat bugs.

Amanda Jane ate them all just the same.

Adam Joshua told Amanda Jane not to stand up in her stroller, and not to crawl under the bushes, and not to throw rocks.

Amanda Jane went right ahead.

"I'm not always going to be around," said

Adam Joshua, pulling his sister out of a rose-bush. "You're going to have to learn to take care of yourself."

"Adam Joshua," Nelson said, pulling his baby out of the rosebush too, "how did we ever get into this?"

———

After lunch, aunts came to visit.

"Watch that tall aunt," Adam Joshua said, pulling Amanda Jane behind him to hide in the closet.

"She's the one who kisses. It's a good thing," he said, "that you've got me."

Amanda Jane started to cry.

"Adam Joshua," said the tall aunt, "what are you doing in this closet with that baby?

"Poor old baby," said the tall aunt, picking up Amanda Jane and kissing her. "Poor old, bad old, sweet old baby," said the aunt, kissing Amanda Jane three more times and carrying her away.

"That kid," said Adam Joshua, all by himself in the closet, "is going to learn to listen to me."

———

"The new wallpaper," said his mother, showing a roll of it to the aunts. The new wallpaper was sunshine yellow with birds and flowers on it.

Amanda Jane crawled over and patted it and drooled on a flower.

"She loves it," said the kissing aunt.

"You'd better watch her," said Adam Joshua. "She'll have it eaten in no time."

Adam Joshua's mother showed the aunts Amanda Jane's new bedroom.

"It's going to turn out lovely," said an aunt, patting a wall.

"Just like her," said another one, kissing Amanda Jane.

"You can see my room too," said Adam Joshua, opening his door.

Aunts, and his mother, and Amanda Jane, went right on by.

"Anytime you want," said Adam Joshua, closing the door again.

———

Later, when Adam Joshua went back to his used-to-be-private room, Amanda Jane was already there. Sticking out of Amanda Jane's mouth were two legs of one of Adam Joshua's Armand's Legion of Space Spies.

"Amanda Jane!" yelled Adam Joshua, pulling the legs out, and going back in for the head.

"Adam Joshua," said his mother, "you stop yelling at that baby!"

Adam Joshua showed his mother the broken Space Spy. He showed her his ripped-up book under Amanda Jane's bed, and his chewed-on poster in the corner.

"Don't just stand there," said Adam Joshua.

"Go get that room finished," he said.

Adam Joshua found a piece of chalk and used it to draw a line across the middle of the floor.

"OK," said Adam Joshua, carrying Amanda Jane over and putting her down on her side of the room.

"Stay there," he said, going back to his half. Amanda Jane crawled right behind him.

"Amanda Jane!" yelled Adam Joshua, showing her the chalk line. "Can't you read?"

Adam Joshua went over to Amanda Jane's side of the room. He took her rabbit, and got her yellow stuffed duck, and picked up a pile of her

clothes. He carried the mobile by putting the string between his teeth. He carried it all into Amanda Jane's new room and stepped over paint buckets and went around a ladder and cleared a space on the floor with his foot, and dropped everything down there.

"Adam Joshua," said his mother from behind him, "you pick all of that up and carry it right back again. We're just not ready yet."

Adam Joshua picked up everything except the mobile and carried it back and dumped it all on Amanda Jane's dresser.

"The mobile too," his mother called.

Adam Joshua got the mobile too and hung it back above Amanda Jane's bed. He gave it a hard twirl.

"Gra-gree-wa," said Amanda Jane, smiling at him and waving from his side of the room.

"Gra-gree-wa yourself," Adam Joshua growled, carrying her back over to her side of the line again.

That night Amanda Jane woke up crying. The only one she woke up was Adam Joshua.

Adam Joshua got out of bed. He took his one-eyed, one-armed, no-legged teddy bear and put it in bed with Amanda Jane and put her arm around it.

"OK," said Adam Joshua, yawning. "Now you go to sleep and stay there." He went back to bed himself.

"Please," he said, falling asleep.

————

"Ready," said Adam Joshua's father.

Adam Joshua went into Amanda Jane's new room and looked around.

Amanda Jane had new soft green carpet the color of the tree outside.

Adam Joshua had a hard wood floor with a chalk mark across it.

Amanda Jane had yellow sunshine walls with birds and flowers on them.

Adam Joshua had dirty white with red things written everywhere.

"It isn't fair," said Adam Joshua, getting his father and showing him the rooms.

"Then you can choose," said his father. "We only had money to do one room this time.

Amanda Jane's too young to care, so you can choose between them."

Adam Joshua chose. He went into the new room and shut the door and sat down in the middle of the floor. He closed his eyes and smelled. He could smell tree-green carpet, and new yellow paint, and fresh new wallpaper with birds and flowers on it.

He lay down on the carpet and it felt like grass, and he looked up at the ceiling and thought about painting clouds and stars there.

"This," said Adam Joshua, "is the perfect room."

He went into his room and shut the door and found a clean place on the floor, beside the chalk mark, and sat down there. He closed his eyes and smelled.

In his old room, Adam Joshua could smell Adam Joshua. He could smell his one-eyed, one-armed, no-legged teddy bear, and his Space Spies, and his new dried worm collection. He could smell the rock Nelson had given him, and the picture from Great-Aunt Emily, and the tree outside the window. He could smell Amanda Jane, and his mother's perfume from when she came to wake him up this morning, and his father from when he came to sit beside the bed last night.

"This room's better," said Adam Joshua, showing his father. "This room's me."

"We'll fix it up when we can," said his father.

"Take your time," said Adam Joshua.

Adam Joshua got the paint ladder from Amanda Jane's new room, and climbed up on it

and drew three stars on his ceiling and a tiny silver sliver of a moon.

He drew a bird on the wall with three flowers around it.

He pulled back the curtains and tucked them up on top, so that the sun coming through the branches of the tree outside his window cast shadows of leaves all over the floor.

"That should do it," said Adam Joshua.

———

"Now we're ready?" asked Adam Joshua's father.

"About time," said Adam Joshua.

Adam Joshua, and his mother, and his father, put Amanda Jane into her crib and pushed it out the door and into her room. They carried clothes, and toys, and the yellow stuffed duck, and the mobile.

When they were done, there was an empty space in Adam Joshua's room with no Amanda Jane in it.

"Good-bye," said Adam Joshua, closing the door.

All by himself, in his own private room, Adam Joshua moved things around. He moved his bed, and he moved his dresser, and he put things in places where he hadn't been able to put them for a long time.

"Need any help?" his father asked, opening the door.

"Not in the least," said Adam Joshua, closing it again.

He rubbed the chalk mark off the floor, and he

sat on Amanda Jane's side of the room until it felt like his again.

———

"Good night," Adam Joshua said, kissing Amanda Jane in her own room. "Don't be afraid here," he said.

He went to get his red marker.

"Don't you even think about it," his mother said, catching him as he went down the hall.

In his own room, Adam Joshua read late because the light wouldn't bother Amanda Jane. In his own room, Adam Joshua played his record player because the music wouldn't bother Amanda Jane.

He went to sleep to stay asleep because Amanda Jane wouldn't bother him.

He woke up.

Adam Joshua lay in his room, wide awake, and listened to see if he could hear Amanda Jane crying.

He listened to see if he could hear Amanda Jane breathing.

"You're lonely," Adam Joshua said, waking up Amanda Jane and carrying her back to his bedroom.

He tucked her in bed safe beside him.

"Now you don't have to worry," Adam Joshua said, falling asleep with his arm around his sister.

"I'm right here," he said.

ABOUT THE AUTHOR

When Janice Lee Smith was five, she told her family in Minneola, Kansas, that she wanted to become a children's book author when she grew up. Now that dream has come true with the publication of her first book for children, THE MONSTER IN THE THIRD DRESSER DRAWER.

Ms. Smith was graduated with high honors from Douglass College of Rutgers University in New Jersey, and received the Edna Herzburg Award for Essay. She was a guest editor with Mademoiselle *magazine and now lives with her husband, James, and their two children, Bryan and Jaymi, in Noblesville, Indiana.*

ABOUT THE ARTIST

Dick Gackenbach has written and illustrated over a score of books, among them HATTIE RABBIT; MOTHER RABBIT'S SON TOM; HATTIE BE QUIET, HATTIE BE GOOD; HATTIE, TOM AND THE CHICKEN WITCH; IDA FANFANNY; *and* MCGOOGAN MOVES THE MIGHTY ROCK.

Besides writing and illustrating, Dick Gackenbach enjoys cooking, dachshunds, classical music, and good books. He currently lives in Washington Depot, Connecticut.

Quirk